To my best girl, Zoe.
—M.A.

To Gemma Murray, with love and hugs.
—S.W.

A Hug for You
Text copyright © 2005 by Margaret Anastas
Illustrations copyright © 2005 by Susan Winter
Manufactured in China by South China Printing Company Ltd.
All rights reserved.
www.harperchildrens.com

Library of Congress Cataloging-in-Publication Data
Anastas, Margaret.
  A hug for you / by Margaret Anastas; pictures by Susan Winter.—1st ed.
     p.   cm.
  Summary: A parent tells a child all of the reasons for well-deserved hugs.
  ISBN 0-06-623613-4 — ISBN 0-06-623614-2 (lib. bdg.)
  [1. Hugging—Fiction. 2. Parent and child—Fiction. 3. Stories in rhyme.] I. Winter, Susan, ill. II. Title.
PZ8.3.A525Hug 2005
[E]—dc22   2003027855
                                                                 CIP
                                                                 AC

Typography by Amelia May Anderson
1 2 3 4 5 6 7 8 9 10
❖
First Edition

A Hug for You

by Margaret Anastas
pictures by Susan Winter

HarperCollins Publishers

A hug for you
on a cold winter day.

A comforting hug
to chase monsters away.

A hug for you.
You're getting so tall.

And another one
for no reason at all.

A hug for you
when you get in a fight,

and you need cheering up
'cause nothing seems right.

A hug for you
when you're sick with the flu.

A blues-chasing hug
when there's nothing to do.

A hug for you.
You sang in the play!

A welcome-home hug

at the end of the day.

A hug for you

when you share with a friend.

When you're losing the race
but you run to the end.

A hug for you.
You wrote your own name!

A good-for-you hug.
You played a great game.

A hug for you!

There are millions, you'll see,
but the best hug of all . . .

is the one you give me.